D0934780

DEAD AIM

DEAD AIM

JOE R. LANSDALE

SUBTERRANEAN PRESS 2013

First Edition

Limited Edition ISBN
978-1-59606-524-6

Trade Hardcover ISBN
978-1-59606-525-3

Subterranean Press
PO Box 190106
Burton, MI 48519

www.subterraneanpress.com

"Too many guns is not like too many guitars."
Hap Collins

EACH TIME OUT, I assume that a job we're hired to do will be exactly what we think it's going to be, and frankly, some are. I don't talk about those much because they're boring. And for a long time I didn't think of myself as a freelance troubleshooter, but instead, a guy looking for work to tide me over until I got my career going, whatever that might be. Then Leonard explained to me that I was actually practicing my profession, and that I was good enough at it and it was really what I wanted to do. That all that stuff about finishing out a degree at my age and becoming a teacher, or some such thing, was just so much talk.

After a short nervous breakdown, and a period of finding my center, as they say in martial arts, I got back on the horse, and now I'm riding, in the dark. But I'm at least on the horse and not being dragged around by it. I realized that Leonard was right. I also realized that like it not, at the bottom of it all, I was a sometime killer.

When Leonard and I accepted a simple protection job, or what seemed simple, I was hoping, as always, that we'd just get it done and go home and Marvin would give us a check that didn't bounce, and we'd be as happy as a stud horse in a corral full of fillies.

A guy named Jim Bob Luke recommended Marvin's agency for the job. It's not exactly a legit job, which is frequently the case. The problem was a lady who had known Jim Bob Luke asked him to help her out. She had an ex-husband who was stalking her, and had actually threatened her, but she couldn't prove it. It was her word against his. Jim Bob was going to be busy and couldn't drive to LaBorde to help out, so he put us onto it.

Me and Leonard drove over to see the lady. She was offering us good money to split between us and the agency. What she wanted us to do, as she put it, was meet up with her husband and have a discussion with him. The way she said it, it sounded like we were just going to set a date at a restaurant and have tea. Of course, that's not what she meant at all.

It was early afternoon in September and some of the hot had gone out of the day. Midday it could get pretty warm in East Texas, but not like a month or so earlier when you could fry an egg on the sidewalk, and going barefoot on cement was like walking across a pancake griddle. It was a pleasant change. Cooler weather was in the offing.

Me and Leonard were the kind of guys that never took anything at face value, or at least we liked to think of ourselves that way. So we thought we'd go over and talk to our client, Mrs. Devon, soon to be the ex-Mrs. Devon, and see if we thought her complaints were legit, or if she was just looking to have someone beat the shit out of her husband for vengeance and entertainment.

From the mouth of the street she lived on, across the way, we could see a new apartment complex, and not far from that was a long street full of fast food joints and doctor's offices and the like. Along the street where she lived, there were a few houses still clinging to the past, like ancient souls waiting silently for death, or hoping for a last visit from somebody before they were knocked down flat and carried out.

Next to those were marginally better houses, pre-fab style, the sort of thing where a shell of a house could be put up in the weekend, and two weeks later plumbing and water would be ready. All that was needed then was furniture, kids to yell at, and a dog to crap on the lawn, which at least for a few months would be a patch of bulldozed red clay.

Mrs. Devon's house was back from the street a bit. There were hedges on either side of her driveway, and they were well-trimmed but a little anemic. In the open garage there was a blue Cadillac that had aged well, and a closed-up barbecue grill pushed up against the wall with a sack of charcoal bricks stacked on top.

We parked behind the Cadillac and got out.

When the door was answered it was by a lady about six feet tall with black hair and a nice shape. She must have been about forty, and you could tell it if you looked real hard, but it was a nice forty, and the body seemed to belong to someone about twenty-five; she obviously had a gym membership, a trainer, and a special diet. She smiled and showed us that she had nice teeth. Her face was nice too. Her eyes were as green as Ireland. When she moved, something primal inside me moved.

After she confirmed we were who she was expecting, we came in and sat down on an elderly but comfortable couch. She asked us if we'd like a drink, and we ended up with ice tea.

"Jim Bob told me you could help me," she said.

"Probably," I said. "I mean, we have to check things out."

"In case I'm lying and just want you to beat up my husband?"

"That would be it," Leonard said.

"He hasn't been all that clever about it," she said. "I don't think he's trying to sneak, it's just that no one has really seen him do anything, or will admit to it. No one but me. I really don't want him arrested. I just want him to stop. The divorce is going to go through, and I don't think he cares about that. He doesn't love me, and I don't love him. He just doesn't like losing me. He wouldn't have minded dumping me. But I dumped him first. That sort of got his panties in a twist."

"When was the last time you saw him?" Leonard asked.

"A few days ago. I had a gentleman over."

"Someone you're dating?" I asked.

"Someone I had one date with. Henry showed up and beat up my date. Bad."

"So there's your proof," I said. "Have your date press charges."

She shook her head. "No. My date wasn't willing to turn him in, because Henry threatened to kill him if he did."

"You think he's capable of that?" I said.

"I don't know. I don't think so. But my date thought so."

"That happened here?" Leonard said.

"Yes. I had left the back door open. I didn't think he was that dangerous. Henry, I mean. But he's big and scary."

"How big is he?" I asked.

"Six-five, maybe three hundred. Not a fat man. Does that scare you?"

"Hell yeah," I said. "But it won't stop us if we believe you."

"All I got is my word, and no one else is talking. I thought I could give you his address and you could just check on him. Follow him around or something, see what you think. See if he shows up here. I've got so I lock all my doors and the windows too. I don't know that he's dangerous, but the beating he gave that man... It was quick and it was awful. I think he may have broken his ribs."

"So he comes by a lot?"

"He used to knock on the door. Now he mostly just drives by, or pulls up in the drive and sits there. By the time I call the cops, he's gone. They've talked to him, but he just says I'm lying, and I can't prove it any other way. They can't post a man twenty-four seven just on my word. And won't. That's why I've come to you."

"Give us his address," I said. "We'll check on him. One of us can stay here with you if you like."

"I have an extra bedroom so one of you can be here all the time. Jim Bob recommended you two and your boss, Mr. Hanson, very highly."

"How do you know Jim Bob?" Leonard asked.

"We dated in high school. I lived in Houston then."

"Jim Bob went to high school," Leonard said. "I thought he came out of the womb the way he is, wearing that hat and driving that old Cadillac."

"That would have been painful for his mother, don't you think?" she said.

"It would," I said. "It certainly would."

"YOU LOCK UP," I said, "and we'll go get a few things we might need, like an axe handle, and we'll be back."

"An axe handle?" she said.

"Call it insurance," Leonard said. "You want the protection, you got to allow us to protect. And discourage."

"You won't kill him, will you?"

"Of course not," I said.

"Look, I really don't want him hurt."

"Only if he tries to hurt us," I said.

"Why don't one of you stay now?" she said. "Start this minute."

"Because we have to decide if we believe you or not."

"Oh."

"In the meantime, lock this place up tighter than a nun's chastity, and we'll be right back."

We walked out and waited for her to lock the door behind us. When we heard the lock click, we walked to the car.

In the car, backing out, I said, "What do you think?"

"Sounds legit," Leonard said. "I think she's scared and wants to get on with her life and wants him to know he's not welcome."

"If we beat the dog shit out of him, you think he'll quit?"

"Hard to say, but I do know it works more often than you hear about. I had someone tell me, you know, you do that, they just come back. I've done it a few times, so have you—"

"And they didn't come back."

"Yep."

"But sometimes they do."

"Yep," Leonard said. "Sometimes they do."

"Henry sounds like he could be pretty hard core."

"Worrying about him being big?" Leonard asked.

"Crossed my mind."

"What the axe handle's for, my boy."

"And if he turns us in for whipping his ass?"

"We were visiting a friend of a friend. That friend being Jim Bob, and she being the friend of that friend. Henry arrived. Violence broke out. Axe handles were lying about, and... Well, you can figure from there."

"And we just happened to be there when he showed up? With axe handles?"

"Exactly," Leonard said. "It doesn't have to be a true story, it just has to be our story... You know, you're getting cautious in your old age."

"I am. I like having a nice home and Brett and a comfortable place to lay my head and put my dick."

"Since I'm living at your house these days," Leonard said, "I like you got a nice home and a comfortable place for me to lay my head, though I'm still in search of a place to lay my dick."

"About that...."

"Yeah. I know," Leonard said. "Like Ben Franklin said, fish and friends smell after three days."

"No. I'm asking about you and John. The dick part, and the deeper meanings that go with it. How are things developing between you two?"

"Nothing much. We talk by phone now and again. I'm almost done with that business. I think you can only brood so long, wait on someone so long, and then you got to move on. But, I'll move out soon enough."

"Not what I meant," I said. "Stay as long as you like."

"Hell, I know that. I was joking. You can't get rid of me."

BRETT WAS OFF on rotation from work. She was sitting at the kitchen table wearing white shorts and a big, loose, red tee-shirt. Her thick red hair was tied back in a bushy ponytail. She wasn't wearing any shoes. Her toenails were painted as red as her hair. She was drinking coffee. Leonard and I went over and poured ourselves a cup from the pot.

"Well?" Brett said.

"We think she's for real," I said.

"So, how are you going to play it?" Brett said.

"Leonard is going to stay there for awhile, and I'm going to be on phone service here at the house. Later, we can swap out."

"What's she look like?"

"She wouldn't hurt anyone's feelings at a glance," I said.

"How about if they concentrated?" she said.

"No one's feelings would be hurt that way either," I said.

"Then you best just let Leonard stay there."

"You're just saying that because I'm queer," Leonard said.

"Exactly," Brett said.

"You don't trust me?" I said.

"I trust you, but I don't know her, and Little Hap likes pussy almost as much as life."

"You know better than that," I said. "Well, you're right about the pussy part and life and all that. But you know what I mean. I'm trustworthy."

"Yeah, but I'm still a little jealous."

We had our coffee, then we got a few things together for Leonard. Toothbrush and toothpaste. Deodorant. Axe handle from the closet. A small hand gun. That kind of stuff.

"Be sure and not shoot anyone," I said.

"Gotcha," Leonard said, got his keys and drove his car away. I watched from the kitchen window until he was out of sight.

"He gone?" Brett asked.

"Yep."

"Great," she said. "Let's screw like mongooses."

WE SCREWED LIKE mongooses and one extra beaver and a water snake, and then lay in bed and watched TV. We watched *Orpheus Rising* on some movie channel. I wanted a cool jacket like Marlon Brando wore in that movie. I knew I'd never have one. Besides, I didn't have anything against reptiles, and it was supposed to be made out of them.

When the movie wrapped, another came on, and we watched part of that, but it wasn't much, and we gave it up. I had a book to read and Brett had a biography. We stacked pillows behind us and lay there nude and read. It was one of our favorite things to do, following the whole mongoose thing, which got number one rating.

Three hours or so later, feeling lazy, I lay down and dozed. Brett woke me, freshly showered, dressed in blue jeans and a blue top, tennis shoes on her feet.

"Baby," she said, "you're taking me out. Get up and shower."

I got up and showered, dressed, and we drove into town to a Mexican restaurant that served a good steak, better than average tacos, tamales, and the usual rice and beans and so far no stomach poisoning. When it comes to good eats, nothing beats Mexican food, though Japanese is close. Sometimes, I eat meat I think about the poor cows, and then I think since I ate them, I might as well wear leather too. No use letting a discarded cow suit go to waste. But I wished I could just eat lettuce and tomatoes and tofu. Doesn't work for me, though. I get sick. Hypoglycemia. I think about a lot of things on a full stomach. It's easier to think about not eating something anymore when you just ate it.

When we got back to the house, Brett pulled on the big loose shirt she had been wearing earlier in the day, and as a treat to me, left off the panties. I pulled on my pajama bottoms as a treat to her, and a loose tee-shirt, and climbed in bed. This was my favorite kind of day. Lazy.

I said, "You said you were jealous earlier, of Sharon Devon. You weren't serious, were you?"

"A little," she said.

"I've never known you to be jealous."

"I didn't think I was. I guess it's because I want to see this arrangement as permanent."

"I already saw it that way."

"I did too, but you know, there were doubts in the back of my mind."

"Because we're not married?"

"That was there in an old fashioned way," she said. "But I don't think that really matters. Not really."

"But it is a braver commitment, isn't it?"

"Maybe," she said.

"Look, honey," I said. "I want to be with you. I'll keep it like it is, or I'll marry you. Whatever, baby. It's you and me."

"You once said something to me about having kids."

"I was just in a mood."

"I think you meant it."

"I did mean it. But, you pointed out what should have been obvious to me; we're a little too old."

"I'm younger than you," she said.

"Everyone thinks you're twenty years younger," I said. "And you look it. Pretty soon they'll be thinking I'm your grandpa."

"That could happen," she said. "But, just in case. I looked into fertilization drugs, you know, to see. Case I might need them."

"I wouldn't want to have a kid just because you think I want one," I said.

"I know that."

"You are a mother, but I've never been a father. I figure I don't become one that might even be best."

"You do know things would change," she said.

I nodded. "I know. And what worries me is—"

"You don't know if you can really change."

"I been trying so long now, that I'm starting to think the trying and not doing it is as much a part of who I am as what I actually end up doing. Which seems to be hitting people in the head, shooting people—"

"And being their rescuer. Hap Collins, have I ever told you that all your doubts about yourself are none of my doubts. That I worry about you using my toothbrush instead of yours, and you sometimes pee on the floor, but as far as your worth as a person, even if you have done some things you consider dark, they do not faze me or concern me at all. Except if we have kids. And it's not about what you're doing, but about what it could do to a child."

"I wouldn't want him or her to grow up like me," I said.

"I would want them to have your integrity," she said.

I started to say something, but it was like a fist was in my throat.

"Let's read," Brett said.

We read a long while, watched the late movie, and then we did the mongoose thing again before going to bed.

When I woke up the next morning, it was to a knock on the bedroom door. I sat up. Brett was gone.

Off to the hospital to nurse someone. Since I was upstairs in our bed, I opened my drawer and took out my revolver and lay back against my pillows.

I said, "Who is it?"

"Marvin."

"Come in."

Marvin opened the door. He hobbled in on his cane and found a chair in the corner.

"How'd you get in?"

"You gave me an emergency key, remember?"

"Is this an emergency?"

"No. But I thought I'd take advantage of my key ownership and see if I could get some coffee. It's nine already."

I put the revolver in the night stand drawer and pulled off the sheets and got out of bed, forgetting I hadn't replaced my pajamas after mine and Brett's mongoose moment last night.

Marvin said, "Oh, the humanity."

DOWNSTAIRS, WITH MY pajama bottoms on, as well as a top, I started the coffee pot. I said, "You don't have coffee at your house? The office?"

"Actually, I forgot to buy coffee for either place. Wife is mad at me."

"Coffee is like a goddamn staple," I said. "You don't forget that. That's just wrong."

"What my wife told me."

"So, what's up besides you being here drinking my coffee?" I said.

"Talked to some cop friends. They said Mrs. Devon reported her husband beating a boyfriend up, and the boyfriend, though he looked like he had been through a meat grinder, wouldn't press charges. Told them he got that way falling down. They didn't have proof otherwise. They think his masculine ego was harmed and he didn't want to harm it anymore by admitting he got his ass beat like a bongo drum."

"So, do the cops believe her ex is bothering her?" I asked.

"They do, but they can't spend all their time waiting for him to show up."

"Course, if he shows up and kills her, they can put their time into that," I said.

"Well, they'll have a pretty good idea who did it. At least solving it will be easy enough."

"There's that," I said.

"Here's the thing, though. They told me if he bothers her, and you're there, don't mess him up too bad, 'cause then you'll be up a creek."

"They know we're watching?"

"Not officially, just my contact at the cop shop. He knows, and he's not telling. But, you mess this guy up too bad, they'll have to look around, and you two may come up in the investigation."

"What's the world coming to that you can't just give a good old fashioned ass-whipping anymore?"

"He's doing what they think he's doing, they want you to whip his ass, just not so much he can make a good stink. If you can find him some place other than her place that would be best."

"May not get to choose," I said.

ABOUT NOON I drove over to Mrs. Devon's house, and parked in the back behind the garage, next to Leonard's car. We weren't being wide open about what we were doing, but we weren't being sneaky either. Sometimes, a stalker isn't a full blown nut, and just the presence of someone who might embarrass them, or put a stop to their actions, can end the matter.

Other times, however, it's worse than that, and what it takes is kicking their asses up under their hair line. Then, sometimes that's not enough. This situation was wide open.

I had been inside the house about five minutes, drinking a cup of coffee offered to me by Mrs. Devon.

I was sitting at the table with her and Leonard and the axe handle, which I had named Agnes.

She said, "Really. I don't want him hurt. I think you should just talk to him."

"That's the plan," I said. "This is just to dissuade six feet and three hundred pounds, if the need should arise."

"I really don't think it will come to that," she said.

I thought she was sounding a lot more confident today. Maybe it was just a good night's sleep.

The doorbell rang.

Mrs. Devon looked at me and Leonard, and we looked at each other. I got up and went to the door and looked through the little square of glass. There was a guy there. He wasn't big. He was carrying a brief case. I didn't take him to be Mr. Devon.

I opened the door. The man looked at me in a kind of stunned manner. "Is Mrs. Devon in?" he asked.

"Who's asking?" I said.

"It's okay," Mrs. Devon said, came over, opened the door wider, unlatched the screen and let the man in. "This is my lawyer, Frank Givens."

She gave him a quick kiss on the cheek and led him into the house and to the table, where he took a seat. I locked the screen back, and then the main door. I sat down in front of my coffee again. Givens was staring at Agnes lying on the table.

"I hope I'm not in the way, Sharon," Givens said.

"Of course not," she said. "This is Hap Collins and Leonard Pine. They are protecting me."

"Has Henry come back?" Givens asked.

"Not yet," she said. "And if he does, my friends here hope to encourage him to leave."

"Being a lawyer I don't know exactly what to say to that."

"We just want to talk to him some," Leonard said. "We can explain someone's position real good, we take a mind to."

"I bet you can," he said.

"They do look like gentlemen who can take care of themselves," Mrs. Devon said, "but then again, Henry is someone who can take care of himself as well."

"Yeah, but there's two of us," I said.

"And we have an axe handle," Leonard said.

"Its name is Agnes," I said.

"Have you seen him yet?" Givens asked.

"No," I said.

"Have you seen those old stills from the silent movie about the Golem?"

"Maybe," I said. "But if I haven't, I get the idea."

"Thing is, he really wants Sharon back," the lawyer said. "Not because he loves her, but because he wants her back. He thinks he owns her."

"Me and Henry were all right for awhile," she said. "I just made a big mistake."

"How long have you been married?" I asked.

"About... What is it, Frank?"

Frank looked as if the answer soured his stomach. "Almost four years."

She patted Frank, the lawyer, on the arm, said, "Me and Frank, we were married once."

"Oh," I said.

"It's all right," she said. "That was some years ago."

I looked at Frank. The look on his face made me feel that he might not think it had been that long ago.

"We were married young," Mrs. Devon said. "We got along fine, but the fire played out. And then I was on my own for awhile, a few years ago I met Henry. He was interesting. Worked in the oil business, and then the business played out, and so did we. I know that sounds terrible. Like it was the money. And maybe it was. We had a nice place, not like here... Oh, I guess this is all right. But we had a nice place, and then the money was gone—"

"And the fire went out," I said.

"Are you being judgmental?" she asked.

"Quoting you," I said.

"You aren't paying us enough to be judgmental," Leonard said.

"Please be respectful," Givens said.

"I didn't mean anything by it," I said. "I'm just saying the fire went out for you, but not for him. I can see you're a woman that could have that effect on someone."

She smiled at me. "You think so?"

"I think so," I said.

She looked at Leonard and smiled. "What do you think?"

"I think heterosexual stuff is confusing to me. I like what men have in their pants, not women."

"Oh," she said. "Oh."

"That bother you?" Leonard said.

"No. No. Not at all. I just didn't know. I mean, you look so masculine... I didn't mean it that way."

"Yeah you did," Leonard said, "but it's all right. Look. The gay folk who fit your idea of gay folk are the ones that stand out. We come from both ends of the spectrum. Some of us even learn how to have sex with heterosexuals and fake a happy orgasm. Mostly those guys are preachers and politicians. Me, I'm a tough guy. Even us queers can make a fist. End of story."

"I assure you, I didn't mean anything by it," she said. "You come highly recommended. The both of you."

Looking at Mrs. Devon I had an idea then why Jim Bob wanted us to do this job. He probably still had the hots for her. She wasn't only good looking, it was the way she talked, the voice, the way her eyes half-closed when she was serious. I even felt a little sorry for Henry then, and Frank Givens the lawyer. I felt like she was a woman that could tell you a sincere lie.

"I can see you're well protected by these gentlemen," Givens said. "That being the case, I'll get right down to business. I have the divorce papers with me. They're all set. He's contesting the divorce, but at this stage, there's nothing he can do to keep you from going through with it. All you need to do is sign."

"But he can be a pain in my ass," she said.

"That he can, Sharon," Givens said.

WE LEFT GIVENS and Mrs. Devon, who we had been told to call Sharon, sitting at the table discussing divorce plans. Me and Leonard went out in the back yard and stood around.

"How about that, Givens is her ex-husband," I said.

"And he still loves her," Leonard said. "And she doesn't even know it."

"Oh, she knows it all right," I said. "I think she's something of a manipulator."

"Starting to doubt her stories about hubby?"

"Not necessarily. I'm just saying she's manipulative. I think she's using Givens to get the kind of deal she wants for very little money. And she might be feeding him a little possibility, if you know what I mean."

"A chance to rekindle the fire."

"Yeah."

"Do we stick with it?" Leonard said.

"So far we don't know things are any different than what she says. But I do have the feeling I'm in a play. A bit actor."

"I know what you mean," Leonard said. "I feel a little played in some way, and I don't even know what it is. But we're getting paid."

"Yeah," I said. "There's that."

"Goes on too long we might have to ask for more money."

I nodded.

"But, if she doesn't offer us any more, and we haven't discouraged her hubby—"

"We'll stay anyway," I said.

"Yep," Leonard said. "It's our way. It's not a good way, but it's the honorable way."

"And it's just about all we got."

"Our honor?"

"No. Our way."

WHAT WE DECIDED was Leonard would stay at the house, as originally planned, and I would try and locate the husband. If I could catch him leaving his place, lurking around Sharon's house, as soon as he acted like a threat, then I'd go after him. Probably after I called Leonard for reinforcements. We're tough, but we're not stupid. Double teaming would be the best system. That way, we could possibly convince Henry the better part of being an asshole was staying at home and minding his own business, letting Sharon go her own path.

Sounded and seemed simple enough.

I had an address for him, and me and Agnes went over there and sat on a hill that looked down a wooded lane. I could see his driveway from there. I sat for a moment and got my shit together, then drove down and past his house and took a look.

The house was pretty nice, but it wasn't well attended. I could understand that. I hated yard work. The front yard was grown up and the trees needed trimming, and it stood out because the houses on either side of his were out of *House Beautiful.*

He had an open carport, and in the carport was a not too old Chevy truck. I drove to the end of the street, to the dead end there, turned around and went back up and sat at the top of the hill. Up there the neighborhood changed, and was not so nice. I parked in the lot of an abandoned laundromat. There were other cars there. It had become a parking spot for the chicken processing plant on the far side of the highway that broke Haven Street, the street Henry lived on.

I had a good view from my parking spot, and nothing was going on down below. I wondered if Henry had a job now that the oil had played out. I wondered if he had money. I wondered if he was as big as they said. I wondered why I was doing this.

I had a CD player with me, and I listened to a CD Leonard had given me, Iris DeMent. It was good stuff. A few years back I wouldn't have listened to it. When I was young I associated country with ignorance and backwoods. The music still carried some of that with it, but no more than what a lot of rap carried with it; when it was ignorant it was urban ignorant. It always depended on who was doing it, and how it was done. I was thinking about that as seriously as if I were going to write a paper on it, when the house I was watching moved. Well, the door did. I saw a man big enough to eat the balls off a bear while it was alive and make it hold its paw against the wound, walk out to the mail box, open the lid and yank out some mail. He was so big I was surprised he could get his hand in there. Frankly, I didn't know people could grow that big. He may have been six-five or six-six, but in that moment he looked seven-six. His shoulders were just a little wider than a beer truck and he was about as thick the other way as City Hall.

We had to deal with that motherfucker we were going to need a bigger boat. Certainly a bigger axe handle. I think we had to graduate to a baseball bat. Maybe a cannon. He might take the axe handle away from us, swallow it, and pull it out of his ass as a sharpened stick with our names tattooed on it.

As I watched him walk back to the house, a little chill went up my back and crawled across my scalp. I pulled out my cell and called Leonard.

"Yeah," Leonard said.

"You know, this Henry guy. I just saw him. He's big."

"How big?"

"Do you remember that robot in *The Day the Earth Stood Still*?"

"Ouch."

"Exactly," I said.

"He still at home?"

"Yep."

"You gonna keep watching?"

"Ever vigilant," I said. "Just wanted you to know what we were up against. And for all we know he's armed."

"You're exaggerating?"

"Nope, I'm being conservative. You know the remake of *The Day the Earth Stood Still*."

"Yeah."

"The robot in that one. More that size."

"Bigger ouch," he said. "Watch yourself?"

"If I want to see something way pretty, that's exactly what I do."

I closed up the phone and put on an old rockabilly CD and listened to that. This went on for hours, me sitting and listening to CD's. I went through everything I had twice, and got so bored I was close to playing with my dick. Then I saw people coming from across the street toward the lot. A bunch of people.

I looked at my watch.

It was quitting time at the chicken plant. Or at least it was a shift change. Pretty soon I'd be the only car in the lot, and that wouldn't be as good. I was considering what to do next, if I needed a new parking spot or what, when I glanced down the street and saw Henry's Chevy pull out of the drive.

I FOLLOWED HIM to a Burger King. He went through the drive-through and I pulled in after him. Looking at his head through the back window, it looked as big as a bowling ball, but with a close haircut.

He made his order, and then I ordered some fries and a big soda, and followed to the checkout window. He went through. I went through. He drove home. I parked again in the abandoned lot. It was just me up there with Agnes, my drink and fries. And of course, my precious thoughts.

Leonard called.

"You want to switch shifts?"

"Nope. I'm fine. I think I'll wait until after dark, then you can drive over and we'll swap out."

I told him exactly where I was parked, and hung up.

I rolled down my window. The air was cool. The mosquitoes however were busy. I was about to roll the window up again when I heard a shot.

I WAS POSITIVE it had come from Henry's house. I had seen a flash of light behind the window. And it was a gunshot. I was certain. I had heard quite a few of them. I thought about just going home or waiting for a neighbor to call, but all the houses were dark on either side of Henry's, and since it wasn't really late, I figured no one was home. If they were, they might not have even recognized what the sound was. Sometimes shots don't sound like much, especially when they come from a small caliber gun.

I had a revolver in my glove box. I got it out. I picked Agnes off the seat and got out of the car. I put the gun under my shirt, in my waistband. I carried

Agnes in my left hand and held her down by my side. The street was pretty dark for the neighborhood. There was no one moving about except a cat, and he didn't seem all that interested.

I went across the street slowly and came up in Henry's yard. I thought I should have called Leonard, but I hadn't. I had just reacted. In the stealth business they call that poor planning.

I took out my phone and turned it off and put it back. All I needed was for it to ring while I was putting on the sneak. I went to the front door and touched it, using my shirt tail to tuck my hand into. No use leaving prints.

The door was locked.

Okay.

I eased around the edge of the house, and now I had my gun out. I was breathing a little heavy. Maybe Henry had fired the shot. Popping a rodent. Didn't like a TV show and was showing it what he thought of it. There could be all kinds of explanations. The one I figured most likely was that someone had shot someone.

Taking a deep breath, I eased my head around the edge of the house, stooping down low to do it. No one was there. The yard was open, with no fence at the back, but there were some thick trees and they went over the hill toward where the highway curved.

I eased around and took a better look. The back door was a sliding glass door. It was open. I went over there on tippy-toes and looked inside. Dark in there. I moved away from the door and leaned against the wall and thought things over. The smart thing was to call Leonard. Or go away. Those were good choices and safe.

Me and my gun and Agnes went inside.

IT WAS DARK and I couldn't see, and I figured if anyone was still in the house, they'd have had time to adjust to the dark. They would be able to see fine. They'd be able to shoot fine.

I leaned against a wall and thought that any moment there would be a shot I wouldn't hear, and it would be all over.

Around the corner from where I leaned was a hallway. There was a break to the left. There was some light in there, but it was the outside light. It was darker in the house than outside.

I moved from my spot, inching carefully into the room beyond the hall. It was a kitchen. A nice kitchen with a nice table and chairs and a coffee pot I could see on the counter, and leaning over the sink, his elbows in it, his knees on the floor, was our big guy Henry.

I said, "Henry?"

Henry didn't call back.

I went over easy, and a little wide. There was a light switch on the wall next to the sink. I used the back of my wrist to flip it on. The top of Henry's head was up against the window sill. He must have been looking out the window when it happened. Maybe at me and my car up there at the parking spot; he might have had my number early on, standing there in the dark seeing what I was doing while someone was coming in to see what he was doing. Someone with a gun. There were brains and blood on the wall and a little on the window, and a lot of it had run down into the sink; most of it had gone down the drain, but as the blood pumped slower, it had started to go thick. He was still big, but that didn't matter much now. You don't get too big for a bullet, if it's placed right.

I didn't shake him to see if he would come around.

I leaned Agnes against the wall, got out my phone and called Leonard.

"Yeah," Leonard said.

"You know that big guy?"

"Uh huh," he said. "Henry."

"We are not going to have to fight him. We are not going to have to deal with him."

Leonard was silent for a moment. "That doesn't sound good."

"Not for him it isn't."

"You hurt him?"

"No."

"Killed him?"

"No. But someone did."

"Shit," Leonard said. "You sure he's dead?"

"Oh, yeah. The splattered brains gave him away."

Lights jumped around outside the window. I took a look. Cop cars.

"My turn to say shit," I said.

"What?" Leonard said.

"I think our donkey is in a ditch."

THE CHIEF OF Police said, "I see you so much, maybe we ought to have a chair put in, something with your name on it, like those movie directors have."

"That would be nice," I said. "Maybe with a built-in drink holder."

We had gotten off the subject, but we had sure been on it a lot for the last hour or so. My butt was tired and I had answered the same question so much it was starting to sound new when I heard it. I was starting to think maybe I should make up new answers. The truth wasn't working.

"Why don't you kind of run over things again," the chief said.

"So you can see if I slip up?"

"That's the idea, yeah."

"I might ought to call for a lawyer."

"You asking for that?" the chief said.

"No, I'm just thinking about it. But, without a lawyer I'm going to say it one more time. I didn't kill him."

"You had a gun on you."

"Weak ploy, Chief. Wrong caliber."

"You can't know that," the chief said.

"I've seen what a gun like mine can do. It would have made a bigger mess."

"Maybe you had another gun."

"Sure. Two gun Hap. What did I do with the other one, hide it up the big guy's ass?"

"We can take a look."

"Go right ahead. There's no one going to stop you. Least of all, Henry. You can prowl around in there all day. Bring the kids."

"All right," the chief said. "I don't think you did it."

"That's nice of you," I said.

"Least not by yourself," he said. "I'm thinking there was you and your partner, Leonard, and he got away. Quick out the back door."

"That's a shitty theory," I said. "He was with Sharon Devon, being a bodyguard."

I had told him all of this, but he liked to pretend we had never discussed it. It's how we danced. I figured Leonard was in another room with someone else, being interrogated same as me.

"So, what's your theory?" he asked.

"My theory is I was there to make sure he didn't bother his soon to be ex-wife."

"And how were you to do this?"

Now we were getting into new territory. "Idea was to keep an eye on him."

"And if he went to see his wife with bad intent?"

"I was supposed to dissuade him."

"And, how pray tell were you supposed to do that?" the chief asked.

"I was going to reason with him. Really, man. We been all over this so many times you could tell me my story."

"Reason with him, huh," he said. "I got to keep coming back to the part about you were in his house and he was dead and you had a gun and an axe handle."

"Sometimes reason requires visual aids," I said.

"Just wrap it up a little," he said, leaning back in his chair, placing his hands behind his head. "Tell me the good part, about how you went in the house and found him like that. Tell me why you went in again."

I sighed. "I was watching the house. I heard a shot. I went down there and went in the back way. The door was open. Henry was hanging on the sink. I think he knew I was following him. Not at that moment. He didn't know anything right then. But before that I think he knew. He made me."

"A clever boy like you?" the chief said.

"Even squirrels fall out of trees. But maybe he was looking up the hill at me in my car. Someone was in the house. They may have come in the back way. The door was open. They snuck up on him."

"That could be Leonard," the chief said.

"But it wasn't," I said.

"You might not have found the door open," he said. "You might have broke in to kill him. The lock had been worked. We could tell from the scratches. A lock kit. You could have come in using that."

"Did you find a lock kit on me?"

"Maybe you stashed it somewhere with the other gun, the one you used to shoot Henry."

"Yeah," I said. "I stuck them both down the commode, along with my spare Range Rover and flushed them."

"Yeah, that doesn't seem so likely," he said. "I think all those things together might cause a clog. I mean, you know, after the Range Rover."

"What was I saying?"

"You heard a shot."

"So, someone slipped in and shot Henry. I heard the shot. I went down there. When I did, whoever killed him saw me. I figure they were in that patch of woods behind the house. They called the cops. It put you on me and off of them, whoever them is."

"The one with the lock pick kit and the right caliber gun?" he said.

"That would be him or her, yes."

"You want a candy bar?"

"What?" I said.

"Candy bar," he said. "I got a couple in the drawer."

"Really?"

He opened his desk drawer and took out two Paydays and put them on the desk. "Go ahead," he said.

I took one and peeled the wrapper off and put it on the desk. "It's a little warm, kind of melted," I said.

"It's free," he said.

"That's true," I said, and took a bite. When I finished chewing, I said, "You don't think I did this, do you? I mean you said you didn't, but really, do you?"

"No, but you're the kind of guy who could do it," he said.

"Shoot him in the back of the head?"

"I think you'd do it anyway you could get it done," he said. "I planned to shoot a guy big as Henry, I'd have shot him in the back of the head. You know, these are pretty good."

"Yeah," I said, and ate the rest of mine.

The chief eased out his breath. "No. I don't think you did it, but it's my job to ask, and I can't treat you any different from anyone else."

"And if you act like you're really on my side, give me a candy bar and all, I'll slip up and tell you something that will hang me."

"It's the sort of thing that's happened," he said.

"But not to me," I said.

"So it's not working?"

"Nope."

"You can go," he said. "But, we might come back around to this again. Same questions. Maybe some new ones to go with it. Could be your answers will change."

"Just restock on candy bars," I said.

I got up and went out.

LEONARD CAME TO the house about an hour later. When he came in I poured him a cup of coffee and put it on the table along with a bag of vanilla cookies.

"I had a candy bar," I said. "Did you?"

"No... They gave you a candy bar?" he said.

"Yep. It's my charm."

"What kind of shit is that?" he said. "They didn't offer me a candy bar. They didn't offer me a fucking stick of gum."

"Did you talk to the chief?"

Leonard shook his head. "I talked to a major asshole who was about five-four and wanted to be six-six, and wished twelve inches of that would be dick. Tell you another thing, I saw Sharon there when I came in, and she looked at me like I had crapped a turd on the tile."

"Yeah?" I said.

"Yeah. And the guy grilling me, he said she rolled over on us."

"They lie like that to get you to give things up," I said.

"I know that, Hap. You think I don't know that?"

"I know you know that," I said. "I'm just saying."

"What I'm telling you though, I saw her there in the hall, and I got the vibes."

"Tell me about the vibes," I said.

"I think we been butt fucked vibes, that's what they were."

"Define butt fucked."

"She had you go over there to watch the guy, and then she had someone go over there and pop him, and guess who takes the rap?"

"They're going to have a hard time proving I shot him with the wrong gun and hit him with an axe handle when I didn't."

"They think she hired you and me to pop him," Leonard said. "That's how it looks, so to help herself out, to make them not think that, she's got to paint us like we went rogue on the deal. Just decided it was easier to lay him down than to follow him around. She may have had it planned that way all along."

"It could be like that," I said. "Though you were at her house."

"But that doesn't do you any good, and she could still make me part of the plan. Say I wasn't there. I could get the rap as the actual shooter."

"She sure seems to be tossing us on the track in front of a train quick-like," I said. "Quick enough you got to wonder."

"Yep... Where's Brett?"

"She picked up a shift for a friend... So what do we do now?"

"I suggest," Leonard said, "we don't let ourselves get screwed any more than we already have. That's what I suggest."

"How do we do that?" I asked.

"I ask questions, as wise men do. I do not provide the answers."

"So, you think I'll come up with something?" I said.

"Probably not," he said. "Why I asked where Brett was."

AT MARVIN'S OFFICE I sat in the chair in front of the desk and Leonard sat on a stool by the counter with the coffee. He had the bag of vanilla wafers with him. He had not offered me or Marvin any, and I was the one who bought them for him. He was sipping a cup of Marvin's bad coffee and eating the wafers. He would put one in his mouth and close his eyes and look as satisfied as a lion with a gazelle in its stomach. If he had had a Dr Pepper, his favorite drink, he would have floated to the ceiling and farted vanilla.

"That doesn't sound good," Marvin said, after I explained it to him. "You know what's worse? She never paid her bill."

"That is the least of our worries," I said.

"It's high on my list," he said. "Hey, I didn't ask you guys to kill him. I just wanted you to do right, get me paid so I could dole out a few bucks to you two. That way, I would have enough for a house payment."

"Funny," I said. "Leonard, think you might want to get in on this? Considering we might go to prison or get a needle in the arm for something we didn't do?"

"I wasn't in the house," Leonard said. "I think I can turn on you and get a lighter sentence."

"And me," Marvin said, "I'm in pretty good shape. I just hired you guys to do a simple observation job. What the lady wanted. And the two of you went crazy. You went in there and shot him with an axe handle, Hap."

"Nice," I said.

"Look here," Marvin said. "Let's figure this thing. Jim Bob knows the lady, so maybe we start with him."

"Nobody knows where he is," I said. "I tried him on the phone before we came here. He's not answering for whatever reason. For now, he's out."

"Then we got to think about what it was we were asked to do. Lady comes in and says she has a recommendation, and it's from one our best buddies, Jim Bob. She says she needs someone to protect her. To discourage someone. We take the job. You guys go over there and talk to her and hear her story and meet her lawyer. How am I doing so far?"

"Good," I said.

"She tells you her husband is big, and it turns out he is. She tells you he is scary and he beat up a boyfriend, a date, whatever. But the guy that got whipped won't press charges. Course, really, he doesn't need to. The cops can go after Henry anyway, if they want. But they think: all right, guy got a beating, wouldn't stand up for himself, so why should we bother? Kind of a Texas thing going there."

"Maybe," I said. "Shit, Leonard. Would you at least not smack?"

"Sorry," Leonard said.

"But whatever, they know he's going to be a shitty witness. Maybe he'll say he fell down a few times and got banged up because he wants to keep his Man Ticket. Won't admit he got a licking. By the way, this guy that took a beating. Who is he?"

I looked at Leonard.

Leonard said, "I don't know."

"Nor do I," I said.

"You know what?" Marvin said. "I think this guy, whoever he is, would be a nice place to start. I think anyone with detective skills would have already thought of that."

"We've been a little preoccupied," I said.

"And you have limited detective skills," Marvin said.

"Well, yeah, there's that," I said.

"Let me show you some detective work," Marvin said.

He called his friend on the force. The one that knew the guy's name. He wrote down the name and gave it to us.

Robert Unslerod.

UNSLEROD LIVED OUT in the country in a trailer. That was surprising. Not the kind of man Sharon Devon would date. Least I didn't think so. She struck me as someone who liked money, a man who wore a tie and took her to good dinners and when he dropped trousers he'd be wearing silk shorts. She was someone that at least wanted a man with a nice car to take her out. The car parked in front of the trailer looked like something the farm pigs drove when they went out for a spin. From the looks of things Unslerod seemed to belong in mine and Leonard's category. He seemed like the sort of guy Sharon Devon would wipe her ass on at best.

We knocked on the trailer door, but no one answered. Maybe Unslerod was actually taking a spin in his Porsche and this is just where he came to store his garbage. When he didn't answer, I got a pad and pen out of my pocket and pressed it against the door to write a note.

The door swung open a little. A smell came out of there that was, to put it mildly, unpleasant.

"Not good, sir," Leonard said.

"Nope."

We went back to the car and stood by it.

"Call the cops?" I said.

"Might just be a dead raccoon under the trailer," Leonard said.

"That stink is from inside the trailer," I said.

"Might be a dead kitty cat inside," Leonard said. "Maybe he went off for the week and forgot to leave Fluffy his kitty food and water dispenser."

"And maybe that's not it at all," I said.

"Yeah, well, probably not," Leonard said, opened the car door and got my revolver out of the glove box and held it by his side. "You get the axe handle."

I got the axe handle. We went back to the trailer and I nudged the door with the toe of my old Tony Lama's. It slid back. I stuck my head around the corner. It was dark in there. The stink was terrible; worse when we got completely inside.

There was a pile in the hallway between the living room and the bedroom, near the open bathroom door. It didn't look like a lump in the rug. It was too big to be a cat.

"Shit," I said.

We went over and looked. It was a man, face down. The floor under him was dark, like a hole had opened up there. He was only wearing dark boxer shorts; my guess was they were not silk. We couldn't tell too much about him there in the dark, but what we could tell was that he wasn't just having a little nap.

Leonard went past me, and holding the revolver in front of him, he looked in the bathroom.

"No one," he said. He went along to the bedroom. The door was cracked. He looked in there. "And the hits just keep on coming."

I went over and looked. There was a nude woman on the bed. There was enough light through the curtains I could tell she wasn't napping either. It was hard to tell what she might have looked like. She was swollen up and her head was bloated. All I could tell was it was a female.

I used my elbow to turn on the light. She didn't look any more identifiable. She looked worse. She was lying on her back with a hole in her forehead. It reminded me of the hole in the back of Henry's head. The sheet under her head was dark and caked with blood. The sheet pulled over her went up to her waist. I was tempted to pull it over her head, but I resisted.

Back in the hall I used the axe handle to turn on the light so we could get a look at the man. He was face down and was stuck to the floor by dried blood.

"Did you touch anything?" Leonard asked.

"The door with the toe of my boot and I used the axe handle on the light. Wait a minute, I put the note paper against the door... I didn't touch anything but the paper though."

"Okay, let's keep it that way."

We went outside and breathed in clean air.

"They been dead awhile," Leonard said.

"No shit, Sherlock."

"And me without my deerstalker."

We got in the car. Leonard put my revolver back in the glove box. I put the axe handle on the back seat.

I said, "I hope no one saw us drive in."

"Probably not," Leonard said. "No houses much. We didn't pass any cars."

It was a good guess. There was only a little dirt road leading to the trailer, and the property was a pasture with high grass and some trees at the back. Still, someone could have watched us turn in. Nothing for it but to hope no one had seen us arrive.

I pulled onto the road and eased along. Driving fast would just draw attention to us.

"This whole business is starting to stink worse than that trailer," Leonard said.

"Yeah," I said. "I'm beginning to feel like you and me have been puppets all along, and that Sharon Devon is our puppeteer."

"Time we cut the strings," Leonard said.

WE WENT TO my place and Brett was home. She was cute in some old overalls worn over a paint-splattered shirt; it had got that way when we repaired a door and painted it. She had the cuffs of the over-alls rolled up and she was barefoot. Her toenails were painted bright red. It went with her hair, which was tied back with a yellow tie. I made some coffee and we told Brett everything we knew. I always told Brett everything I knew. The only people I would tell that sort of thing were her and Leonard, maybe Marvin. Under certain circumstances, Jim Bob. In fact, when I got through telling Brett all we knew, she said, "Seems like you got to start with who put you in her camp."

"Jim Bob," she said.

"Makes sense," I said, "and maybe we can do that, but I got to say, if we were fooled, Jim Bob was fooled. And on top of that, I have tried him, without luck. He's not answering his phone. I figure he's turned it off on purpose. He may be in the middle of a job, and the kind of work he does often means the cell is off."

"I wasn't saying he had anything to do with it," she said. "Just that he might give you some insight."

"Yeah, he and Devon used to date," Leonard said.

"Way back," I said. "What I figure is she may have always been selfish, and over time, she became more of that. A whole lot of that. Enough so that it might lead to something that had to do with murder. Jim Bob, if he hadn't seen her in awhile, he wouldn't know that. Wouldn't suspect it. He'd remember her as the woman he dated."

"Problem with that," Leonard said, "is I was with her when Henry was killed. And somehow I can't see her breaking into that trailer and popping Unslerod and his girlfriend."

"Yeah," I said. "I figure whoever picked Henry's lock picked the trailer lock, caught Unslerod heading for the bathroom, shot him, and was in the bedroom before the woman knew what happened. They were probably both dead in less than fifteen seconds. If it took that long. Wouldn't have to be a professional killer, but someone who knew locks and was sneaky as an alley cat."

"Or professional," Leonard said. "I'm voting professional, but I'll settle it could be either way."

"Maybe you guys ought to forget all this," Brett said. "You're off the job. Not your problem, really. Maybe you stay out of it she won't try to pin it on you."

"I don't want to feel like I let her set me up and she got away with it," I said. "Or that I somehow helped any plan she had all along to kill Henry. I don't know how I helped, but I have this horrible feeling I did. We only got how bad Henry was from her. Unslerod, what did he do? What did his woman do? I don't like it."

"You know what?" Leonard said. "Actually, we didn't just hear how bad Henry was from her. We heard it from the lawyer."

"And he's still in love with her," I said.

"Bingo," Leonard said. "You got any more cookies?"

Brett got up.

I said, "Don't show him the stash."

She laughed and opened a drawer next to the sink. It had two bags of vanilla cookies in it.

"And you know what, hon," she said to Leonard, "I got you some Dr Peppers."

"Oh, hell," Leonard said. "I swear, darling, I am going to quit being queer and go straight so I can take you away from Hap and you can keep me supplied in cookies and Dr Peppers."

LEONARD WAS TAKING a nap on the couch, and Brett was upstairs in bed reading. I turned on the computer in Leonard's bedroom we had built onto the house for him, and did some checking on Frank the lawyer. What I got was Frank's firm had been around a while. He owned it and employed other lawyers; in other words, he ran a large aquarium for sharks. I looked to find out about his cases, discovered his firm was pretty good. They had nice odds on their winnings. Not too many losses. They did everything from divorce to murder trials, but they didn't seem to be ambulance chasers. As far as I could tell, they didn't advertise on TV. They had been around long enough they didn't have to. I called Marvin, told him what I found, asked if he might be able to find out more from some of his contacts. "After all," I said, "as you have pointed out, you are the detective."

"An attempt at flattery?"

"How's it working?"

"I see it coming as clearly as an elephant trying to walk a high wire, so not so well."

"But, then again, aren't you the true detective?"

"Damn you, Hap Collins," he said. "It is working. You have found my weak spot."

I went upstairs and locked the door and took off my clothes and slid under the sheets with Brett. She was sitting up in bed with pillows at her back. She had the sheet pulled up over her. She had her reading glasses on, pushed down on her nose. She put the book in her lap.

"I hope you don't think you're going to get any?" she said.

"Any what?" I said.

"Don't act coy with me," she said.

"I just got naked," I said. "It has nothing to do with you. I'm comfortable naked. Some of us are quite comfortable with our bodies, our nudity."

"Oh," she said.

"Yep."

"I'm reading, you know."

"How's the book?"

"Sucks."

"So, want to do the nasty?"

"That is far from romantic," she said. "But lucky for you I think a lot of that stuff is nonsense. The romantic stuff. I'm not as girly as I look. And then again, the book sucks, so that makes your suggestion a little more interesting."

"Dear, believe me," I said. "You are as girly as you need to be."

She laid the book on the bed beside her. She dropped the sheet. She was naked too.

"Surprise," she said.

THE PHONE CALL woke me up. Brett stirred in my arms.

"You get that," she said.

I slipped loose of her and put my feet on the floor and picked up the phone. It was Marvin.

"You busy," he asked.

"Not right now," I said.

"This Henry guy," he said. "He seems to have been a pretty straight dude. Made a lot of money in oil. He was a land speculator for the companies. His job was to get people to give up beautiful land so it could have trees cleared, the soil torn up by a bulldozer, concrete and oil drills put down. He made a lot of money. And then he didn't."

"It comes and goes," I said.

"People were drilling everywhere because of the oil shortage talk, and then when they drilled in some places and didn't find as much as they hoped, they quit drilling so much."

"And he quit making money," I said.

"But here's some things," Marvin said. "He has a daughter. Her name is Nora. My cop friends say she has been arrested. A lot. Mostly stupid stuff. Small amounts of drugs. Being at the wrong place at the wrong time with the wrong people. Not exactly a Bonnie Parker, more just troublesome. Lindsay Lohan without the fame and without that much money. Daddy had enough money to help her out of deep doo-doo, though, until he didn't."

"So what has she got to do with this?" I said.

"I'm not sure," Marvin said. "Maybe nothing. But she didn't get mentioned by Sharon Devon, did she?"

"Nope. The girl didn't come up in conversation," I said.

"My friend at the cop shop said Sharon and Henry always came down together to bail her out and such, and that it was pretty clear to them that the girl was close to Sharon. Like a mother. Her actual mother was dead. Car accident. Got an engine block through the chest."

"So, you're saying why didn't the dog bark in the nighttime?" I said.

"That's right. If they had a daughter and were divorcing, and the daughter was close to them both, why didn't she come up in your conversation with Mrs. Devon? And where is she? She was supposed to be living with Henry. The cops have been looking for her too, and nothing. No one knows what happened to her."

"Connected?"

"Maybe," Marvin said. "Cops have tried to find her every which way, but it's like she fell off the face of the earth. I'm not sure what that means or what we should do, but something about it bothers me."

"The lawyer," I said.

"What do you mean?"

"I mean I figure he knows something more than we know and we ought to know it."

"Lawyers have client privilege," Marvin said.

"Sometimes that wavers if they think you're going to beat the hell out of them," I said. "Not saying we would, but maybe he could think we mean to, even if we don't say we plan to. Just sort of insinuate."

"Maybe we ought to just drop it," Marvin said. "A reason we ought to, and I have been holding this back for dramatic effect, is Sharon Devon went down to the station and said she didn't think you had anything to do with Henry's death, and that she sent you there, and you were only doing what she asked."

"That's kind of different than before," I said.

"I guess she thought about it," Marvin said.

"Or decided she didn't need that dodge anymore."

"Well, there's a little bit more," Marvin said. "She's got a big insurance policy. Henry left everything to her and he's got this policy that's worth about seven hundred and fifty thousand dollars. They weren't divorced, and he hadn't changed his will or his policy, so it all goes to her."

"So she didn't have any reason to make too much of a stink about us being involved," I said.

"It clears the palate some," Marvin said. "It gets attention away from her, and it's just another unsolved murder. And there's all that money. Maybe not as much as he would have had a few years back, but it's more than starter change."

"You think she had him hit?" I said.

"It happens," he said, "but if so, why hire us in the first place?"

"It made Henry look like a bad man and it made us look like someone who might have put him down, and it confused the situation. It doesn't seem to take much confusion to mess a jury up these days. If she could plant in people's mind that he was dangerous, any sympathy there might be for him could be negated."

"You sound like you're holding something back, Hap," Marvin said. "It's not what you're saying, but I know your tone well enough to know there's something missing here."

"Not really," I said. "I was going to get around to telling you. Maybe, like you, I was holding it back for dramatic effect. I meant to tell you earlier, but I wanted to think about things first. Unslerod, you remember him?"

"The guy that got beat up by Henry," Marvin said.

"He's dead, and a woman who was with him is dead too."

"Shit."

"I haven't called about it. I figured they weren't going to get any deader. Maybe stinkier, but not deader."

I gave Marvin the location of the trailer. That way he could contact his friend at the department, maybe keep me and Leonard out of it. Marvin too.

"This is getting more complicated," Marvin said.

"Still think we should let it go?" I asked.

"I think we ought to," Marvin said. "And I want to."

"But we won't, will we?"

"Of course not," Marvin said.

I had no sooner got off the phone than there was a knock on the bedroom door.

Leonard called out, "I woke up and I was all alone and I didn't know where you were."

"Go fuck yourself," I said.

"Get up and let him in," Brett said.

I got up and pulled on my pajama pants and tee-shirt, unlocked the door and let Leonard in.

"The cookies are missing," Leonard said.

"I put them up," I said. "You eat all of them if I don't hide them. You'll have a tummy ache."

"You hid Leonard's cookies?" Brett said. She was sitting up in bed with the sheet pulled around her. Her red hair fell against the white sheets and her fine skin and made her look like a goddess.

"They're not his cookies," I said.

"Are too," Leonard said.

"Yeah," Brett said. "They are. You go down there and give the baby his cookies."

I said, "You're spoiling him, you know."

WHEN THE LAWYER, Givens, came out of the restaurant, we were waiting in the parking lot. We had followed him from his work and parked as near to his car as possible. We had been waiting all morning for him to leave his office, not even sure he would, but hoping eventually he'd come out. If he went to lunch we could maybe pull off talking to him easier than trying to set a time at his work and him not wanting to talk to us; we tried it that way, he could avoid us for ages. So, when he left we were watching from across the street and we followed him, and now, here we were, waiting.

While he was in the restaurant enjoying a good meal, Leonard and I were eating hotdogs from Sonic, which frankly, wasn't half bad.

We ate and waited, and after about hour he came out. As he got close to my car we got out and started walking like we were going into the restaurant. He looked up from fumbling with his car keys and saw us.

"Hello," he said, and gave us one of those smiles you would expect from someone who had just discovered his zipper was down.

"Hey," I said, like it was a big surprise to see him. "How are you?"

"Okay. Just grabbing a little lunch."

"Yeah, well, good," I said. "We thought we'd have a little lunch ourselves."

"That's nice," he said. He couldn't have been more awkward than if he were standing on a mile-long razor blade over a gorge.

"You know, things really didn't work out for us on that gig with Ms. Devon," Leonard said.

"Yes, of course," he said. "I know. Sorry about that."

He tried to dart for his car.

I said, "Thing is, we think a lot of what happened stinks. We think maybe we got played for fools."

"I'm sure you're mistaken," he said.

"Then you wouldn't mind talking to us?" I said.

"Did you follow me here?" he asked.

"Happy coincidence," Leonard said.

"Well, I don't know I have anything to say," he said. "Ms. Devon is my client, and—"

"Oh, come on," I said. "It's just us guys talking here. She's more than a client."

"She's also a friend," he said.

"Ah," Leonard said, "I bet you feel more than that for her. I mean, hell, you were married to her for awhile, and to think that big jock Henry was riding her around the bedroom like she was a pony had to get your goat."

"That is inappropriate," Givens said.

"So is framing our ass," Leonard said.

"Ms. Devon has made it clear you had nothing to do with what happened," Givens said. "It was just an unfortunate coincidence."

"Coincidence, huh?" Leonard said. "You know what I'm thinking, and I'm just thinking here—"

"And for him to do that, he has to really be serious," I said, "because it hurts his head."

"There you have it," Leonard said. "But I'm thinking since you knew Hap was watching Henry's house, you sneaked over there and picked the lock and shot Henry. Hap hears the shot, like maybe you thought he would, and he comes in and looks bad for it."

"I already told you Ms. Devon says it was a coincidence, and the police believe her."

"That's good," I said. "Really, but we still got to wonder if that was part of the original plan, to have our dicks mashed between two bricks."

"I didn't shoot anyone. I don't even own a gun, and I don't know how to pick locks, and if I were going to frame someone, I'd find a better way to do it than that. Hoping you heard a shot and came in and got framed. That's not a very good plan."

"It wouldn't have mattered if I came in," I said. "All that mattered was I was there, and the cops could fill in the rest of the blanks."

"Wouldn't you have to have the same kind of gun that killed him?" Givens said. "Wouldn't you have to have a gun that had been fired?"

"Okay," I said, "you're starting to sound more convincing. Listen, let me put it another way. We really don't know you had anything to do with it. We're just fishing. But we don't like being played for idiots. Some might think that happens daily, but they would be wrong. Leonard just looks foolish, he's not."

"Thanks," Leonard said. "That was mighty white of you."

Givens said, "Good day," and made like a bullet for his car.

I trailed after him. When he got to the car, unlocked it and was opening the door, I said, "Thing is, if you two have something going on that's got nothing to do with us, maybe we can help. Maybe you ought to talk to us."

Givens looked back at me, paused. I thought for a minute he was going to say something, but instead he got in his car and drove away.

"He hesitated," Leonard said. "I think that help line got to him."

"I was just throwing it out there, seeing if it had a hook on it."

"I think it did," Leonard said. "And some bait, and he almost went for it. That makes me think maybe he's telling the truth. Or part of the truth. That they didn't set us up. But it's also got me thinking he knows more about what happened than he's letting on."

"I keep telling myself if we're out of it, we ought to let it go," I said.

"I know," Leonard said. "But you know, that would be a first, and I'm not sure I want to start down that road. Next thing, I'll break down and buy my own cookies. And you know that ain't right."

WE HAD JUST pulled away from the restaurant when my cell rang.

It was Marvin. He said, "I got a call from Givens."

I had it on speaker, so Leonard heard it. "That was quick."

"So, does this mean we're in trouble," I said.

"No," Marvin said. "I think something you did may have worked out. He wants to see you at his office, downtown in an hour. It's a pleasant request. He even said please and that he's thought over what you said and he wants to talk straight."

"Interesting," I said.

"Find out how interesting."

We stopped by Starbucks and sat at a table and had coffee in mugs. Since I found out you can have it in a ceramic mug if you don't plan on carrying it off, I had it that way every chance I got. It tastes better.

We drank our coffee, and then went over to the law office and rode the elevator up to the third floor. When we got there the office door was open. Frank Givens and Sharon Devon were both there. Sharon was in a chair near the desk. She looked as if she had just seen her own ghost.

Givens was standing up behind his desk. As we came in, he said, "Shut the door."

I shut it.

"I started to say something in the restaurant lot," Givens said, "but you see, part of the problem was who I had lunch with today. I wanted to get out of there as swiftly as possible. Before he came out. I didn't have your number, so I called your boss."

"Sometime boss," Leonard said. "Actually, he can't do without us."

"So you weren't there to eat?" I said.

"I lied," Givens said. "I went in and I sat in a back booth in a conference room and got talked to by a person who is part of the problem. Him and his bodyguard."

I looked at Leonard, said, "Is any of this making any sense?"

"Not to me," he said. "But I'm still trying to figure out the ending to the Sopranos."

"I'm sorry," Givens said. "Please sit down."

There were two very comfortable leather chairs, and we sat in them.

Sharon Devon had not spoken a word. She looked as if she had been crying. Her eyes were red as sunrise and she looked more her age today, as if she had finally lost the war against it. I felt sorry for her. I feel sorry for just about everybody.

"We led you along some," she said.

"Figured that," Leonard said.

"Me and Henry," Sharon said, "we weren't really having trouble."

"Okay," I said.

"We were just pretending," she said.

I glanced at Givens. He didn't look too happy. I couldn't tell if it was about Henry and her not actually having trouble, or about something worse. I decided a little of column A and a little of column B. I had a suspicion there might even be a column C.

"So we were just sort of window dressing?" Leonard said.

She nodded. "Yes. You see, we have a daughter, Nora."

We knew that, of course, but we didn't say so.

"She is by Henry's previous marriage. I was never able to have children. But, I love her quite a bit. Nora was precious to me. She wasn't quite a teenager when we first met, but I took to her right away, and she to me. After that came the teenage years and Nora was pretty wild. Not that uncommon. I was pretty unruly myself. Nora started seeing boys we didn't want her to see, and she started experimenting with drinking and drugs. It made what happened later easy." She paused. Givens got up, went to a cabinet and pulled out a bottle of water, got a glass and a coaster and brought it over to her. He placed the glass on the coaster and unscrewed the cap on the water bottle and poured about half a glass.

Patiently, she waited while he did all this, as if a pause like this was the most natural thing in the world. For the two of them, maybe it was. When he was finished she sipped her water, delicately, placed the glass back on the coaster.

"You see, Henry really was in oil," she said. "And he really did have a loss of money. But part of the reason wasn't just a shift in natural fortune. There was a dismantling of fortune, and Henry was the cause. He liked to gamble. He liked to gamble a lot. Then the business went bad and he got into debt with the wrong people. He bet on some football games, some horses. He bet on just about anything. He would have bet on the number of freckles on my ass if I'd have been willing to let someone count.

"I loved him, but he was a gambling addict, and no matter how bad the people were he got into debt with, he kept letting the debt get deeper. Then they put interest on what he owed. Lots of interest. About double. They wanted him to get in deep, because they assumed he was a big shot, and that whatever problem he was having paying would go away, because they had had a few ups and downs with him before, and in the end, he had paid it off, and with interest. Lots of interest."

"But the downs didn't stop," I said.

She shook her head. "No. They didn't. He went to them and told them there was no way he could pay all that back if they kept compounding the interest, which they were doing. They didn't listen. He was late, so they added on a late fee, and added interest on that. He told them if they stopped compounding it, maybe he could pay it back, in time. He probably couldn't have paid it back if they had let him go back in time to the beginnings of the earth and work it off up until now. The business, it wasn't coming back. Not the way they thought it might. Fact was, he had lost the business, but they didn't know that."

Sharon paused and drank some more of her water.

"He let them think he was still making money. Maybe that was the right thing, to let them think that, because if they didn't think he could pay, they didn't have any reason to let him live. They even threatened me. We had some money. But it was just eating money, gas, enough to pay a few bills. We didn't have enough to pay them so that it would mean anything to them. That's when we came up with a plan. Idea was we'd divorce and sell the house."

"I don't see why you would have to divorce," I said. "Don't see the plan in that."

"Turns out it wasn't too good a plan," she said. "We tried to get clever because we thought we were smarter than a bunch of thugs."

"You probably are smarter," I said, "but not as clever. They're two different things."

"Or as ruthless," Leonard said. "That's something makes them real different."

"Why didn't you just go to the cops?" I said.

"For the same reason I said," Sharon said. "We thought we were smarter. We didn't want people to know about Henry's gambling debts. We thought we could work things out and no one would know, and we could make some kind of life together again."

"So what was the plan?" Leonard said.

Sharon drank more of the water and looked as if she might break out crying. She didn't. She said, "Thing was, Henry thought if we were divorced, at least they'd leave me alone. They didn't. And the man that I said I dated, that got beat up—"

"Let me guess," I said. "He isn't really your type."

"No," she said. "He was a messenger for the people Henry owed."

"And Henry beat him up, causing more problems," Leonard said.

"Yes," she said, "but there was already a problem. You see, the messenger came to my house because he said he wanted us to know that if we didn't pay he had our daughter. She had been seeing someone that was part of the problem. Jackie Cox. She was in with the wolves already."

"Ah, I got it," I said. "The Dixie Mafia Cox family."

"You know them?" she said.

I shook my head. "I know who they are. They took the place of someone who used to run this area's business. Those people we did know. They came to kind of a sad end."

"Rumor is," said the lawyer, "you were involved."

"Rumors are all over the place," I said.

"Jimson and his crew," the lawyer said, "they got killed in a filling station in No Enterprise, and the rumor is from cops I know, you and Leonard might have had something to do with that."

"We had our problems with Jimson," I said. "But no. That wasn't us."

And it wasn't. It was a young and lethal lady named Vanilla Ride who had put them down, but that's a different story.

I said, "I don't want you to be too disappointed about that, though. Me and Leonard, we've had our moments, and I figure you wouldn't have asked us here if you didn't know that, and didn't want us to have a moment again."

"Jackie was seeing our daughter," Sharon said. "She met him because of my husband and his gambling dealings. He didn't intentionally introduce her to Jackie, but he used to have these tough guys coming around, and Jackie, he's the son of one of them."

"Richard Cox," I said.

She nodded her head. "They got tight quick. Maybe because he was a bad boy, and Nora liked bad boys. But then Henry owed them the money, things went bad, and then they sent this Unslerod around."

"He was kind of a tough guy they used," Givens said.

I didn't mention that he wasn't that tough anymore, and unless Marvin got in touch with his cop friend, Unslerod and his girlfriend were still collecting flies in a trailer out in the boonies.

"He said they had our daughter," Sharon said, "and if Henry didn't find some way to pay half, soon, and the other half almost as soon, they would harm her. Henry was already living apart from me, trying to set the divorce up to maybe make me safer, and then this guy came around. He was looking to talk to Henry. He thought he was tough."

"But Henry was tougher," I said.

"Much more so," she said. "He gave him a beating and they didn't get any money. It was a foolish thing to do, them having our daughter. I don't think Henry believed them at first. Then they sent this."

She opened her purse and took out a plastic bag and dug in the bag. When she got through with that she pulled out another plastic bag and unwrapped that. There was a pair of red thong underwear inside.

"These are hers," she said. "I bought them for her and her father didn't like that I did. All the girls were wearing them, she said, and I thought it was harmless. Anyway, they're hers. I know they are. It proves to me they have her."

"What we would like," Givens said, "is that you go and get her back. That you make these men stop bothering Sharon. They killed her husband and took her daughter, and now they're pressuring her to pay. She can't pay. They have come through me with all this. They said Sharon goes to the cops, or doesn't pay something on what she owes, and by something they mean a substantial amount, they will send the part of her daughter that fits in the underwear to her in a cardboard box with a bow on it."

"How much time did they give you?" Leonard asked.

"Three days," Givens said, without waiting for her to answer.

AT MARVIN'S OFFICE, he said, "So, how do you read it?"

"I think Henry got his dick in a crack," I said, "and he was too arrogant to take care of matters when he could, so he just kept it there and the crack got tighter. He didn't pay, so they took his daughter. They sent around a guy they thought was tough to collect and tell Henry how things were, that being Unslerod, and maybe he thought he'd play tough on Henry. Henry was tougher. Maybe Unslerod pissed Cox off with his failure, or maybe it was some other reason, but it seems more than likely Cox had him taken care of. His girlfriend was probably just in the wrong place at the wrong time. Later on it was Henry's turn. I figure Unslerod and the woman were dead some days before Henry, considering how their bodies looked. Way I understand it, Cox doesn't like failure, and he gives it a very short shelf life."

"Question comes to me," Marvin said, "guy owes you, why whack him if you want the money that bad?"

"That's the question me and Hap got to thinking on coming over here," Leonard said. "We got to thinking on it hard enough that I cell phoned Sharon. I asked her how they expected her to pay what was owed, and she said—"

"Insurance money," Marvin said, and snapped his fingers at the same time.

"Yep," Leonard said. "You are a wizard. She has a shit-full policy. Seven hundred thousand. Henry managed to keep that up, as protection for Sharon. That isn't even all Henry owes, but it's a good part of it. She told me that, I cleverly asked, doesn't it take time for the policy to pay out? And she said it did, and you know what?"

"The lawyer is helping her out," Marvin said, leaned back in his desk chair and placed his hands behind his head. "He's going to put the money up for her in return for the insurance money."

"Yep," Leonard said. "He's not only an ex-husband carrying a torch, he's a fucking saint."

"Sure he is," Marvin said. "Sure he is."

WE DROVE OVER in my car and met the lawyer. We were going to go with him to the Dixie Mafia guy and they were going to give us the girl in exchange for the lawyer's money. When the insurance paid off, Givens was going to get his money back from Sharon. He was carrying a briefcase when he came outside his office and met us at the curb.

It was a nice day, and I wondered, as I often wondered, if it might be my last day on earth; if this might be the day I set out to do something simple and it turned bad and I'd end up in a ditch with crows pecking at my eyes.

Givens climbed in the back seat with his briefcase. He said, "We got to drive to Tyler."

"All right," I said, and I slipped away from the curb. "We meeting in the city?"

"That's the plan," he said. "It should go easy enough."

"They explained it to you?" Leonard said. "You got all the particulars down?"

"They just want the money," Givens said.

"What about the boyfriend?" I said. "Cox's son?"

"He was just the bait," Given said. "He was the one that got her to trust him."

"And that's kind of what we are, aren't we?" I said.

Givens was quiet for a long moment. "I don't think I follow you."

"I might have to throw a few words in, but I figure you'll put it together pretty quick. I'm talking about you getting us to trust you, same as you say Jackie did with Nora."

Givens didn't say anything. I looked at his face in the rearview mirror. He was doing a fair job of looking puzzled.

"Let me see the briefcase," Leonard said.

"Why?" Givens said. He put a hand on top of it where it rested on the seat.

"Because if you don't," Leonard said, "I'm going to have Hap pull over by the side of the road and I'm going to kick your ass so hard you'll be peeking out of your asshole."

"What in the hell is wrong with you guys?" he said.

"Let's just say we don't like your story," I said, "We look in the suitcase, see the money there, we might believe you better."

"It's there," he said.

"Show it to us," Leonard said. "And right now. I'm feeling edgy."

"He wanted vanilla cookies," I said, "but he got up too late, and I had eaten all of them with my coffee. You don't want to make him mad when he hasn't had his cookies."

Givens had no idea what his life had to do with vanilla cookies, and frankly, neither did I, but it was on my mind. Cookies are not cheap, I'll have you know. Not when your brother eats them by the bagful. What really made me mad was Leonard didn't gain a pound. I looked at cookies too long and I could feel myself gaining weight.

Leonard leaned over the seat and held out his hand, said, "And that gun you got under your coat. I saw it when you got in the car. Reach for it and I'll be over this seat pronto and stick it up your nose."

"I just brought it for safety," he said.

"But you told us they said not to bring guns," I said. "They making like a special deal just for you?"

"Hand me the case," Leonard said. "While you're at it, hand me the gun. Never mind."

Leonard went over the seat and was on top of Givens so fast Givens probably thought Leonard had a warp drive up his ass. I glanced in the mirror. Leonard was practically sitting in Givens' lap. He reached the gun from under Givens' suit coat and threw it in the front passenger's seat. Then he slapped Givens across the face, twice, fast as the beat of hummingbird's wings, then got off Givens' lap and picked up the briefcase. Givens held his hand to his mouth as blood dribbled between his fingers.

"You didn't have to do that," Givens said.

"I thought I did," Leonard said. "Soon as I saw that bulge in your coat, I knew you'd lied to us, that you were putting our lives in danger by bringing your gun, or that there was more to things than you wanted us to know."

"Another thing," I said, "just for the record, we brought guns ourselves. Because, you know what? We didn't believe you. First, you're a lawyer, and that's a mark against you, and second, you still got a thing for

Sharon, and third, you putting up that kind of jack for your former wife seems unlikely, love her or not. You may be a lying scum bag lawyer who makes a lot of jack, but it's hard to think even you got seven hundred and fifty thousand just lying around? Possible, not likely. So, that means you got something else going on here. Something that might even make you look like a bit of a hero, and we would be there to witness you turning the money over and taking the girl back. That could ingratiate you to Sharon, couldn't it?"

"We don't do this right," Givens said, "it'll turn out bad. Real bad."

Leonard opened the briefcase. "Well, now, ain't this some shit," he said.

Leonard turned the case toward me. It only had a pile of empty manila folders inside.

"That won't pass for money," I said.

"No," Leonard said. "It won't."

I pulled over to the side of the road and put the car in park and looked back over the seat at Givens.

"Lay it out," I said. "No stalling. No stories within stories. Lay it out."

"NO ONE WAS meant to get hurt," Givens said.

"Yeah," I said, "it's all fun and games till someone loses an eye."

"Henry owed the money, and well, I know the people involved. You might say I handle their affairs."

"You're their lawyer," I said. "The Cox family."

"That, among other things."

"That's goddamn typical," Leonard said.

"I do odds and ends for them here and there. Henry owed them and they wanted their money, and they knew I knew Sharon and that I had been married to her."

"Favor time," I said.

"Yeah," he said. "They wanted me to put the screws on her to make Henry give up the money. I thought if we had someone threaten Henry he'd give it up. I was sure he had money in some hidden account somewhere. They sent Unslerod around and he didn't work out so well."

"Henry turned out to be tougher than they thought," I said.

"He did," Givens said. "Then Unslerod decided he'd blackmail me by threatening to let Sharon know I worked for the organization."

"The organization," Leonard said. "I like that. The Dixie Mafia and Cox you mean."

Givens nodded.

"That meant you had to get rid of Unslerod," Leonard said. "And when you did, the woman just happened to be there."

"Something like that," Givens said, and I saw in his eyes then something that made me shiver a little. He may have been a frightened weasel, but I knew in that moment I had to keep my eye on him. Because nothing is more dangerous than a frightened weasel. They have no loyalties but themselves.

"That was cold," Leonard said.

"He was a deadly man," Givens said.

"But not so deadly you couldn't sneak up on him and shoot him," I said. "And then the woman."

"It just worked out that way," Givens said. "I used a credit card on the door and I surprised him. Well, he surprised me too. I shot him, and then I went in the bedroom and she was there and I didn't have any choice. I shot her too."

"No choice, huh?" I said.

"I didn't think so," Givens said.

"So what happened next?" I said. "Better yet, let's go back in time to Nora."

"I didn't want to do that, but I set it up so Jackie could meet Nora. He got her interested in him, and then she moved in with him."

"She wasn't kidnapped?" Leonard said.

"No," Givens said, sighing so loud it was like a wind storm blew into the car. "What I thought was it could look like a kidnapping. Cox said that would be good, and his boy Jackie was for it. And so was Nora."

"Nora was in on it?" I said.

"Yeah," he said. "She was. Big time. Way we arranged it was we'd hold her for ransom and Henry would come through. Like I said, we all thought he had money and was holding back, and that if he thought Nora was in danger he'd give it up."

"Only problem was he didn't really have any money," I said.

"Correct," Givens said. "No money. Or at least I don't think so now. He loved Nora. I think he would have come through if he had any."

"So you revised the plan, and the revised plan included bad things for Henry," Leonard said.

"I didn't so much revise it because I wanted to, but because I had to. Cox had one of his men do in Henry. A black guy named Speed. He's big as Henry, but more dangerous."

"Let me guess the rest," I said. "You told them they had to do Henry because you knew about the insurance policy. You never planned to give Cox your money until you got the policy money. You'd just pretend to take Sharon off the hook. Me and Leonard would be there as witnesses, and you'd hand them the suitcase full of folders, and they would give you Nora, and you would bring her home like she was let go, and when the money came through, you'd give it to Cox because he liked the plan and didn't mind temporary ownership of

folders and a briefcase. When you paid them the insurance money, minus you and Nora taking a little off the
top for your troubles, no one would be the wiser."

"It wasn't all that Henry owed," Givens said. "But
it was enough for them to be satisfied, and it would
take Sharon out of the mix."

"And you'd look real good in her eyes," I said.

He nodded. "I suppose that's true."

"You and Nora are some pair," I said. "Nora cheating her grieving stepmother for some dollars and for
this Jackie Cox, and then you cheating Sharon. Not to
mention committing murder."

"That's pretty much it," Givens said.

"You know," I said. "One revision on what I said
earlier. I don't think you brought us along so we
could say what a hero you were. I think you brought
us along because Sharon insisted. She said she wanted
us along to make sure things went well. She wanted us
to protect you and Nora. How am I doing?"

"All right, I guess," Givens said.

"You know what, Givens," Leonard said. "I didn't
check you out so good. I see you are trying slowly to
ease your hand down to your sock, where I suspect,
just under your pants leg is a holstered hand gun that
you hope to pull and shoot me and Hap with."

Leonard poked the gun he had gotten off the
front seat against the side of the lawyer's well combed

hair, just over his temple. "What you want to do is tug up your pants leg, pinch the gun out by the grip with thumb and forefinger, and hand it to me easy as if it might blow up."

Givens did as he was told. Leonard took the gun. He tossed it over the seat into the passenger seat and hit Givens across the head with his own gun, right over the ear. It knocked Givens sideways. He reached up and held his head. When he moved his hand there was blood on his fingers.

"You sonofabitch," Givens said.

"And don't you forget it," Leonard said.

I had some tissues in the car and I gave some to Givens and had him wipe the blood off his head and hand.

"What we're going to do," I said, "is we're going to go through with this plan. Almost. We're going to have you waltz in there with the briefcase. We're going to have you be a really nice guy and not let on we know dick about what you're doing, 'cause if you do, we will kill you deader than a tree stump.

"When we get the girl, both of you get a drive to the police station. We'll call Marvin and have him grease the path for us with the cops. We'll turn you and her over to them, let you figure out how to explain extortion, illegal gambling profits, murder, and fraud, or whatever the fuck crimes we got here. Thing is, we play this right, we get you two and they get the brief-case, thinking they're going to get insurance money later, and you get to leave without a hole in your head. How's that plan?"

"Cox won't forget," Givens said.

"We'll see how that turns out," I said. "We got long memories ourselves."

Givens didn't say anything. I figured he didn't like the plan.

THE MEETING PLACE was on the first floor of a two-floor parking garage in Tyler. Just before we got there we pulled over and Leonard made Givens get up front in the passenger seat, and he sat directly behind him. He had both of Givens' guns and one of his own he had brought, and I had mine from the glove box tucked in a holster at the small of my back, with my shirt pulled down over it.

When we drove inside the garage we went to spot 15, as Givens said for us to do. A big black car—of course it was black—was waiting. We pulled up behind it and a man got out. He was an exceptionally large black man that moved like a cat; frankly he moved the way Leonard and I do. I'm just telling it like it is. One bad man can spot another, even if that bad man is me and I'm feeling a lot less bad these days. I figured he was the aforementioned Speed. He was dressed in an expensive black shirt, coat, pants, shoes, and a very glossy black dress jacket that couldn't have been off the rack, not and fit those shoulders. His head was shaved and it looked to have been waxed. It was shiny enough you could have used it as a mirror to comb your hair.

"You go on and get out," Leonard said to Givens. "I'd be real cool, I was you."

Leonard got out, and Givens got out.

Speed looked at me behind the wheel. He was expressionless, which was expression enough. Guy like that, not showing much in his features, you had to watch him. Wasn't the kind of fella that would give you many signals before he shot or punched you or drove a car over your ass.

I had my window rolled down. I said, "Hey, how's it hanging?"

Speed ignored me. He looked at Leonard and Givens. They had come around to the front of the car.

"Givens," the big man said.

"Speed," Givens said.

"Hey," Leonard said. "How about this weather?"

"Which bozo is this?" Speed asked.

"Leonard," Givens said. "Guy behind the wheel is Hap."

"How's it hanging," I said again.

Still no evaluation of the general hanging condition of his meat was offered by Speed.

"Here's the thing," Speed said. "You got no guns, right?"

"Not exactly," Leonard said. "I actually got some guns."

Speed turned his attention to Givens. "You were told no guns."

"They go their own way," Givens said.

"That's right," Leonard said. "Way I see it, since we're all pals we won't be shooting anybody, right? You came with a gun, because I see it under your well cut coat."

"You don't leave the guns," Speed said, "we don't go."

"How about we get where we're going, we all put our guns in a pile," I said. "Till then we keep them. You see, the lawyer here told us your rules, but we're here to make sure he don't get shot and we don't either. To make sure it works out that way, we got to have rules of our own. One of which is we hang onto our guns until it looks like it's okay to let go of them."

I knew that since this was scam, there was no real threat in saying we wouldn't give them the briefcase. Cox wanted the meeting to happen, to set it up so Givens could give him the insurance money eventually.

It was a big joke, but a joke only works if you play it right. Thing was, they didn't know we were in on the joke. We had a few laughs of our own planned.

Speed let what I said move around in his thoughts for a while. His expression didn't change.

"You follow me out," he said.

He got back in his car and we backed out from behind him. He pulled from his parking place and drove off. We followed. I saw that he was on his cell already.

WHEN BAD GUYS start directing you outside of town it's always a crap shoot. But that's where we were going, outside of town. We passed what used to be Owen Town. It was really nothing more than an asphalt path and a couple of storage buildings. It had never been a town since I was alive, but it used to be a place where aluminum chairs were made. I worked there when I was young.

We went along until we came to the cutoff for Starrville, a little burg so small most of the inhabitants could have lived in one house, and maybe a shed out back. We didn't go all the way there. Instead, we stopped in the Starrville Cemetery. There was another black car like the one Speed was driving already parked there. The windows were dark. A man got out from behind the wheel. He was a big white guy with a crew cut. He was almost as big as Speed. His jacket, an ugly plaid thing, fit him the way a designer dress fits a hippopotamus.

Speed got out of his car. We got out of ours. After a moment, the back door of the other car opened and a man slid out, leaving the door open. It was Cox. I had never met him, but had seen a couple photos of him on the internet; usually something to do with law-breaking. He always claimed to be innocent, and always got out of whatever problem he was in. He was a tall, lean man with gray, well-cut hair, and a look about him that said he liked things his way. He was dressed in a nice gray suit to go with the hair. My dad always told me not to trust anyone who ran around in the middle of the day with a suit on. If they wore one because they were on their way to preach, he told me to watch them even closer.

"So," said Cox, "we're here to deal."

"If you got something to deal with," I said.

"They got guns," Speed said.

Cox glanced at Speed. "What did I tell you?"

"No guns," Speed said, but he didn't look worried about the situation. My guess is it was mostly show. My bet is when I saw Speed was on his cell phone he was calling ahead to tell Cox we had guns.

"We just want to play even," I said. "Your man here has a gun. And I'm going to guess the guy in the plaid coat has one too. Wouldn't surprise me you had one. All I'm saying is we all keep our guns and stay friends. Having us put ours up and you keeping yours, that wouldn't be playing fair. And me, I'm all about fair play."

"You said we would put them all in a pile," Speed said.

"I lied," I said.

"All right," Cox said. "We'll play your way." He looked at Givens. "Got the money?"

Givens held up the briefcase they both knew was empty.

"Good," Cox said.

"You got the girl," Leonard said.

"I do," Cox said.

He looked back at the car. A young man who looked a lot like Cox, but with black hair, got out. He poked his hand back inside the car, when he pulled on it, a girl came out with it. She was dressed in jeans and a tee-shirt. She wasn't wearing a bra. This wasn't a negative. She had un-real red hair and a pretty face, but there was something about it that made you want to throw a pie at it.

Givens said, "These men, they know what the real deal is."

I looked at Leonard. He looked at me. The cat had just jumped from the bag.

Givens walked over to Cox's car carrying the brief-case. He stood by Cox.

"They know," he said. "They know and they're trying to work me to get the girl back. They know she's in on it."

"Yeah," Cox said, "and how do they know that? You tell them?"

"They figured it," Givens said.

"That's right," Leonard said, "we're pretty smart for old country boys. We can even tie a square knot in the dark."

I let my hand drift to the edge of my shirt. Speed eased his coat back. I think the guy in plaid was still trying to figure out what everyone had said. Cox didn't look any different at all. Oh, maybe a bit irritated, but nothing more. The girl looked at the young man, who I figured was Jackie, then looked at Cox. She seemed to be waiting for someone to tell her something.

"All right, so they know," Cox said.

"They plan on taking me and her to the police," Givens said.

"They do, do they?" Cox said.

"That's exactly the plan," Leonard said.

No one said anything for a while. A plane flew over. I wished they were parachuting in reinforcements.

"I think there's more of us than there are of you two," Cox said.

"What a mathematician," Leonard said.

"Me and Leonard get to shooting though, your numbers may decrease," I said.

"Speed here," Cox said, "he's fast on the draw, and he hits what he aims at."

"I'm not that fast on the draw," Leonard said, "and I'm not that good of a shot, but I still might hit something. But him, Hap, he can shoot. That motherfucker is a natural. He don't really know from guns, but he knows shooting. It's like a goddamn inborn knack."

"This is true," I said. "I'm like a fucking prodigy."

I didn't add that my expertise was really with long guns, though I did all right with a handgun. And Leonard was right. I didn't know that much about the workings of guns, really. Not the way gun nuts do; the guys talking about them the way you ought to talk about a woman, but I could hit stuff. As for fast on the draw, I had no idea. I never thought of slapping leather with anyone. I usually had my gun out and ready.

"We got quite the conundrum then, don't we?" Cox said, and grinned a little.

"Pretty conundrummy," Leonard said.

Speed was a little to my left rear, but I could see him well enough. Across the way was Crew Cut, and not far from him were Cox and the girl, Jackie and Givens. Leonard was off to my right.

"You know what?" Leonard said. "I'm going to step a little wide, in case my man here decides to shoot. He's got dead aim, but I don't want to be in the line of fire. He might let a lot of bullets go."

"You really good?" Speed asked me.

"There's all manner of opinions floating around," I said.

"He will blow your head off, Speed," Leonard said, without looking back at me, keeping his eyes on the others. "It will happen so fast you'll never know you have a hole in you."

I thought: Don't build it up so much, Leonard. This Speed guy, he looks like someone who would like to try me out, and I'd rather not. But I didn't let on I was worried. I smiled a lot. I was one confident and happy looking sonofabitch.

"I'm thinking I might like to try you, fast man," Speed said.

Shit. I knew it.

"We don't have to, you know," I said.

"You sound a little scared," Speed said.

"It's just I don't like having to clean my gun," I said. "All that smoke in the barrel. The cost of a bullet."

"You know what I think," Speed said, pushing his coat back so the butt of his holstered gun could be seen. "I don't think you're that—"

I drew and wheeled and shot him, right in the center of the chest. I wheeled again, toward Crew Cut. He was struggling his gun out of the holster beneath his coat. I shot him in the arm. The gun he'd grabbed went flipping away and he fell back against the car, grabbed his arm, said, "Shit."

Leonard had his gun out now. It was about time.

"Damn, Hap," Leonard said. "That was some good shooting."

"Wasn't bad," I said. "Disarm the dick cheese."

Leonard pointed his gun at them. He said, "You, Nora, you get their guns from them, bring them over here and toss them on the ground behind the car. You get feisty, I'll put a hole in you. I got a rule, anyone tries to hurt me gets hurt, male, female, wild animal. And if they got hide-out guns, those better come out slow and easy too, not be hanging around for later. Something like that would make me irritable, and like the Hulk, you wouldn't like me when I'm mad."

Nora did as she was told. It was quite a pile of guns she dumped behind the car. When she was finished, Leonard said to her, "You come over here and get in our car. Sit in the backseat, put your hands in your lap and look prim."

Nora got in the back seat of the car the way a child in trouble will do.

I went over to Speed. I had been watching him carefully ever since he hit the ground, except for when I shot the crew cut fellow. He was bleeding badly and his eyes were blinking very fast. He wasn't even trying to reach for his gun. I knelt down beside him.

"Damn, my man," Speed said, coughing a little. "I never even cleared leather."

"That's because I'm faster than you," I said.

Speed made a barking laugh that tossed blood onto his lips. "You're the real deal," he said.

"Frankly," I said, "I didn't know that until just now."

I pulled his gun from its holster, just in case he might be stronger than he looked, though the way he lay there he gave the impression that lifting his fingers would be a serious workout. I lifted his head up so he wouldn't choke on his blood. I turned my head, said to the young man: "Your name is Jackie, right?"

He nodded.

"You have the sports coat man there give you his coat."

"My arm hurts," Crew Cut said. "And I like this coat."

"Give him the coat anyway," I said, "or you won't have to worry about hurting."

Jackie went over and Crew Cut worked his way out of the coat. Jackie brought the coat to me. He said, "Don't hurt Nora. This wasn't any of her idea."

"I don't believe that," I said, "but she isn't going to get hurt as long as she doesn't get cute. Now, sit down there on the ground in front of my car."

Jackie went over and did just that. I rolled the coat up and put it under Speed's head.

"Bullet didn't have much impact," Speed said, still gurgling blood.

"It was enough," I said.

"I mean I didn't feel it so much," he said. "But I can hardly move."

"That's because you haven't had time to feel it," I said. "Now shut up. You're spitting blood."

Speed lay quietly on the sports coat.

I got out my cell phone and made a call.

NEXT DAY WE were at Marvin's office, in our usual spots. Marvin behind his desk, me in the chair in front of it, Leonard sitting by the coffee machine, munching on vanilla wafers. At least he had bought those with his own money.

Marvin said, "I called you here to tell you the cops believe your story, about how you thought you were just getting the girl back and they tried to kill you, so you shot them. They're not too happy about you going out there without calling them, not telling them what the deal was, but I think they're in a forgiving mood. They been wanting Cox on something that would stick, and you two talking at a trial, and Givens talking to save his own bacon, that'll nail him. And way I figure it is you'll be all right 'cause they'll be shit-blind happy you helped nail Cox."

"What about Speed?" I said.

"They think he's going to make it and get to go to prison," Marvin said. "He appears to be as tough as boot leather."

"But he's not near as fast as he thought he was," Leonard said. "My man here is like fucking Wild Bill Hickock."

"I got lucky," I said. "And I shot him while he was talking."

"Well," Marvin said, "I think his future career is wood shop in prison."

"What about Nora?" I asked.

"The kid, Jackie, he's saying she didn't know anything about it, and so's the old man. She's gone back to her stepmother. I think the cops will let that stand. Givens will get some time too. He's backing Jackie's story about the girl having nothing to do with it. Guess he wanted to have the same story Cox had. He's helping put Cox in prison, but maybe he didn't want to go the whole hog, thinks he might get a brownie point or two."

"Think he will?" I asked.

"Nope," Marvin said. "They will most likely have him shanked in prison. They do, no tears here."

Leonard said, "Me either."

I have to admit, I didn't see myself shedding tears for that lying, conniving weasel.

"I believe Nora thought she found true love," I said, "and would get some money out of her father, and she'd have some teenage revenge on her step-mother. For what, I'm not sure, but it seems that's how she was thinking. She was close to her, but maybe she got unclose when she started to grow up and thought Daddy was putting more attention into Sharon than her. No idea really."

"Frankly," Leonard said, "my take is she's just stupid. Probably glad it's over, probably glad to be home. Probably forget Jackie in a year's time. You can bet the way she'll tell it to Sharon is she was forced. I think that little shit's a born liar. One of those entitled turds who think they have the best of everything coming just because they are who they think they are, not necessarily who they are."

"That's some serious psychoanalyst shit going on there," I said.

"Naw," Leonard said. "I just sort of made that up."

"Actually, that's what I really thought," I said.

"I think that's what Sharon wants her to do; just pretend things are fine between them until they are," Leonard said. "In the long run, I think she figures what really happened won't matter, and she's probably right. And maybe Nora really did find true love, because Jackie didn't tell it different, and Cox didn't say his son was lying, so you got to give the old man points for going with what his son said. I think the cops want to let Nora go. They got the fish they wanted to fry, and could care less about the minnows."

"Cox family values," I said. "Kind of touching. Go figure."

BRETT AND I were lying in bed. I said, "I love you."

Brett turned and put her arm across my chest. "I love you too."

"I asked you to marry me, would you? Right now, if I asked?"

"Are you asking?"

"I'm running a test," I said.

"A test, huh," Brett said.

"Yeah."

"I don't know, baby. Really, I don't. I want to, but you know, I got married once before and it ended with me setting my husband's head on fire."

"So, you get married, you have to go for gasoline and a match?"

She laughed.

"No, I'm just saying what happened before, my first attempt at wedded bliss. What I'd say about us is this. Let's give it some thought. Let's see if it's something that really matters, and if it does, we'll get past talking about it. Maybe we'll decide things are just fine the way they are and we don't need a piece of paper."

"It's not the paper, it's the commitment."

"I know. I'm just saying let's think about how much it matters to us. Give it some thought, some time."

"All right," I said.

"Do you want to play doctor?"

"No," I said. "I'd just like to hold you."

"Really?" she said.

"Really."

"That works too," Brett said, and so I held her.